T0380844

Drake
And The
Ducks

Janice Sabulsky

Print information available on the last page

Rev. date: 12/21/2018

To order additional copies of this book, contact:
Xlibris
1-888-795-4274
www.Xlibris.com
Orders@Xlibris.com

One day, Mateus's Grandma
came home and said to
Mateus's Grandpa,
"Look, a lady gave me a box of
baby ducks."

"Why do you want a box of
baby ducks, that is crazy!"
said Mateus's Grandpa.

"The ducks have been wandering alone for two days. They are cold and weak.

I will take care of them," said Grandma.

Grandma gave the ducks a bath
in a big blue bowl.

They already knew how to swim
and really liked the water.

Uncle Mike brought a nice big cage to Grandma's house.

He helped set the cage up on the deck.

Grandma and Uncle Mike put
the ducks in the cage with a
dish of food and some water.

The ducks had such nice
brown eyes.

When Grandma touched them
with her fingers
they felt very soft.

The ducks all took turns splashing in the bath tub.

Sometimes, they would all try to jump in at the same time.

Drake was the oldest duck.

He would always look around
to make sure it was safe for the
other ducks.

When the ducks got tired,
Drake would tell them that it
was nap time.
They would all snuggle
together in
a big bowl.

Drake told Mateus's Grandma
that they liked living at
her house.

The ducks liked to be out on
the deck so they could
feel the warm sunshine on
their faces.

As the ducks got bigger,
Grandma got them a wide
flower pot to cuddle in.

Sometimes they would try to
climb in at the same time and
they would knock it over.

When the cage got too small, Mateus's Grandpa made a playpen cage. Drake showed the others how to find food on the ground.

Freddy, the big black dog would watch the ducks through the bars of the playpen.

Can you see Freddy?
He is trying to hide.

Romeo, the silly hound dog,
was scared of the ducks.

He was afraid they would bite
his long ears.

One day, Drake told Grandma that the ducks were almost all grown up and would like to find a nice pond to live in.

"We are wild ducks", said Drake, "we don't want to live in a cage anymore, it makes us sad."

"You are right", said
Grandma," it is time to find
you a real home.

Wild ducks belong in a big
pond. I can see that you are
sad in the cage."

Grandpa got in his big red truck
and went looking for
a nice pond just for the ducks.

The next day, Grandma put the ducks in the cage one last time for the trip to the pond.

They were so big now that they hardly fit in the cage.

Drake and the ducks sat in the cage on Grandma's lap. Drake looked up at Grandma and said," I can hardly wait to see the pond!"

When they all got to the big
pond Grandma said,
"This is so beautiful, the
ducks will really like it here."

Grandpa put the cage on the ground and opened the door.

There were so many new sounds and smells at the pond.

At first, the ducks were a little bit scared.

Drake told the others, "Wait here for a minute, I will check it out."

"It's great," he shouted to the others, "let's go for a swim." They all walked to the edge of the pond and looked in.

Drake swam out and told the others, "come into the water-there are lots of good things to eat in this pond."

They ate and swam for
a long time.
They could stretch their legs
and feet all the way back in
the water.

They splashed their wings in
the water.
Drake showed the others how
fast he could move
across the pond.

Grandpa watched them and
smoked his pipe.

Grandma sat on a stump and
took pictures of the
beautiful pond.

Drake and the ducks found a
fun corner to explore.
There was a little tunnel that
they could swim into.

They played hide and seek.

Can you see the ducks?
They are hiding.

Finally, Drake swam over to Grandma and said, "It is nice here. We will be very happy.

Thank you for taking care of us when we were little and all alone."

"I will miss you", said Grandma.
We will come back and
visit you soon."

And they did.

This book has been created
for our grandson
Mateus Michael Soares

May you always love to read and learn
new things.

May the wonders of nature always
hold you in awe.

Special thanks to Sharon Kalischuk who followed the baby ducks
for two days, protecting them from predators and making sure they
were really alone before taking them from the wild.

Printed in the United States
By Bookmasters